D1459996

Piero della Francesca, Giovanni Bellini, Perugino, Fra Angelico, Andrea Mantegna,
Domenico Ghirlandaio, Masaccio, Pietro and Ambrogio Lorenzetti, Fräulein Gasterstädt,
thank you and sorry.

—V. R.

To E. R.

the Mighty Asparagus

by V. Radunsky, who believes with all his heart that this is a true story, although some people may doubt it, still he believes that it is true.

MANUFACTURED IN CHINA

These are the people who made sure that everything in the story makes sense, checked the grammar, verified that all pictures are printed nicely, and all because they also believe that this story is true.

An amazing asparagus grew right in the middle of the king's yard. One day, there was nothing there, and on the next unfortunate day—there it was. That morning, the king came out for a walk and...

"Oh, my!
In my own backyard.
That thing...Amazing!"

It wasn't that he was so happy to see it (as a matter of fact, he wasn't too fond of asparagus), but it was amazing, don't you think? And that's exactly what he said: "Oh, what a mighty asparagus! Amazing!" The king's advisers (remarkably wise people) also looked and said, "Amazing..."

"No, no, no," the king said.
"This is too ugly.
It sticks out like a sore thumb.
This won't do. I must get rid of this monster at once."
And the king gripped it just like so.

But...nothing happened. The mighty asparagus didn't even budge. The only thing that did happen was that something (could have been an eagle, I am not sure), already nestled somewhere on the top, made a frightened squeak. Spooky!

"Oh, I hate that stinky asparagus!"

said the king, and he went to find his queen.

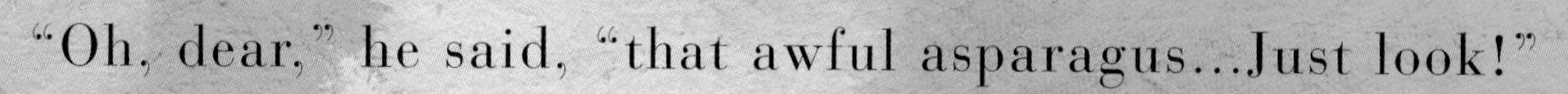
"Oh, dear," he said, "that awful asparagus...Just look!"

"No, dear, it's beautiful! What might!

I want to bring it to the palace. I want to own it.

I want to admire it all day long," said the queen.

The queen hugged the asparagus tightly. Like this.

The king hugged the queen tightly. Like this.

And together they pulled with all their might. Like this.

But nothing happened.

Do you remember that I told you about the king's advisers (remarkably wise people)? Once again they looked at each other and said,

"Amazing! What a mighty asparagus!
What a mighty asparagus it is!"

The king said, "I know. Let's bring my favorite of favorites, my beloved rhinoceros. He is very strong and very mean. He will help us."
The queen said, "I know. Let's bring our bravest knight.
He will be sure to help us." And then...

Oh, I almost forgot. How silly of me. The king and the queen had a daughter, the princess.

The princess squealed, "I am hungry. Give it to me now! I want to gobble it up!"*

*Funny. I thought that children hated asparagus. On the other hand, maybe princesses are the only children who like asparagus. I don't know.

Then things happened like this.
The princess was shouting,
"Hurry! Hurry! You, Knight,
you stand on top of the rhino.
We'll tie this here.
You, Papa, hold Rhino's tail.
You, Mama, you pull here.
And I will shout at the top of
my lungs!

One, two, three.
Let's go!"

"Humph . . . Hrrmph . . . Ayah . . . Oy . . . Poof . . ."

The rhino also said something, but it was absolutely impossible to tell what it was.

And then? Nothing.
Nothing happened.

Well, something did happen....
You are not going to believe it.
I am not even sure that it is true.
But they say that the king burst
into tears, howling,

"Mom! Mo-o-ma! Mo-o-o-o-m!"

Of course the king had a mother.
What do you think?
Here she is.
She looked exactly like this.
Well, almost exactly.

"Mom!
I can't do it,"
said the king.
The mother said, "You all go to the garden...Not you, Rhino. You stay there. Then ask Tiny Little Bird, who sings so sweetly, to help us."
"And then?"
"And then you will see."

And then the king did exactly as his mother said. He tied Tiny Little Bird to the mighty, mighty asparagus. Tiny Little Bird had barely fluttered its little wings. And?

And the humongous, stupendous, splendid, catastrophic vegetable collapsed! What a noise it made.

One lady said
I don't understand why they had to pull it out. It wasn't in anyone's way and it was beautiful to look at.
Here I must say I disagree. It's better that it was pulled out.
And somebody said
You should always listen to your mother.

Amazing...
Amazing...

And one person even said
Even the smallest effort counts.
I think these are truly beautiful words!
And some people were musing
Such a huge asparagus it was, and now it's fallen and beaten down. And people are walking all over it.

And still others were saying
Isn't it wonderful that we have such a wonderful king and queen, such a wonderfully strong and mean rhino, such a wonderfully strong and brave knight, and such wonderfully wise advisers?
And the king, of course, was happy and proud.
I must be a wise and brave king after all. I should ask my advisers about that.

And the king's musicians even composed a song. A ballad.
It was called "The Ballad of the Mighty Asparagus."
I remember the melody went like this: "Tra-la-la-la-la,
tra-la-la-la-la..." That should be sung high. And then low,
"Tru-lu-lu-lu-lu, tru-lu-lu-lu-lu..."
A very beautiful ballad.

O asparagus, mighty asparagus,
O asparagus that would not fall.

O asparagus, mighty asparagus…
Etc.

The End

Library of Congress Cataloging-in-Publication Data Radunsky, Vladimir. The mighty asparagus/by Vladimir Radunsky. p. cm. "Silver Whistle." [1. Asparagus—Fiction. 2. Kings, queens, rulers, etc.—Fiction. 3. Birds—Fiction.] I. Title. PZ7.R1226Mi 2004 [E]—dc22 2003012241

ISBN 0-15-216743-9

Book design by Vladimir Radunsky Prepress by B-Side Studio Grafico, Roma
Color separations by Bright Arts Ltd., Hong Kong Manufactured by South China Printing Company, Ltd., China
This book was printed on totally chlorine-free Stora Enso Matte paper.
Production supervision by Sandra Grebenar and Pascha Gerlinger
First edition H G F E D C B A